STATE PROFILES
UTAH

BY EMILY ROSE OACHS

BELLWETHER MEDIA • MINNEAPOLIS, MN

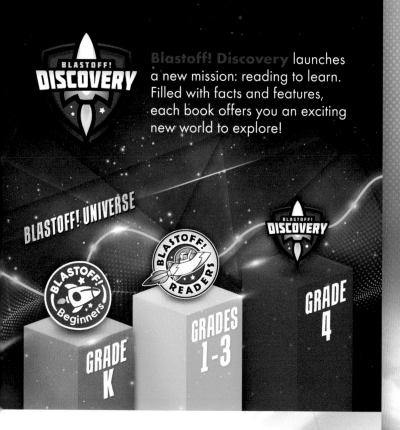

Blastoff! Discovery launches a new mission: reading to learn. Filled with facts and features, each book offers you an exciting new world to explore!

BLASTOFF! UNIVERSE

BLASTOFF! Beginners — GRADE K

BLASTOFF! READERS — GRADES 1-3

BLASTOFF! DISCOVERY — GRADE 4

This edition first published in 2022 by Bellwether Media, Inc.

No part of this publication may be reproduced in whole or in part without written permission of the publisher.
For information regarding permission, write to Bellwether Media, Inc.,
Attention: Permissions Department,
6012 Blue Circle Drive, Minnetonka, MN 55343.

Library of Congress Cataloging-in-Publication Data

Names: Oachs, Emily Rose, author.
Title: Utah / by Emily Rose Oachs.
Description: Minneapolis, MN : Bellwether Media,Inc., 2022. |
    Series: Blastoff! Discovery: State profiles | Includes bibliographical
    references and index. | Audience: Ages 7-13 | Audience: Grades
    4-6 | Summary: "Engaging images accompany information about
    Utah. The combination of high-interest subject matter and narrative
    text is intended for students in grades 3 through 8"
    – Provided by publisher.
Identifiers: LCCN 2021020866 (print) | LCCN 2021020867 (ebook)
    | ISBN 9781644873502 (library binding) |
    ISBN 9781648341939 (ebook)
Subjects: LCSH: Utah–Juvenile literature.
Classification: LCC F826.3 .O25 2022 (print) | LCC F826.3
    (ebook) | DDC 979.2–dc23
LC record available at https://lccn.loc.gov/2021020866
LC ebook record available at https://lccn.loc.gov/2021020867

Editor: Christina Leaf   Designer: Laura Sowers

Printed in the United States of America, North Mankato, MN.

TABLE OF CONTENTS

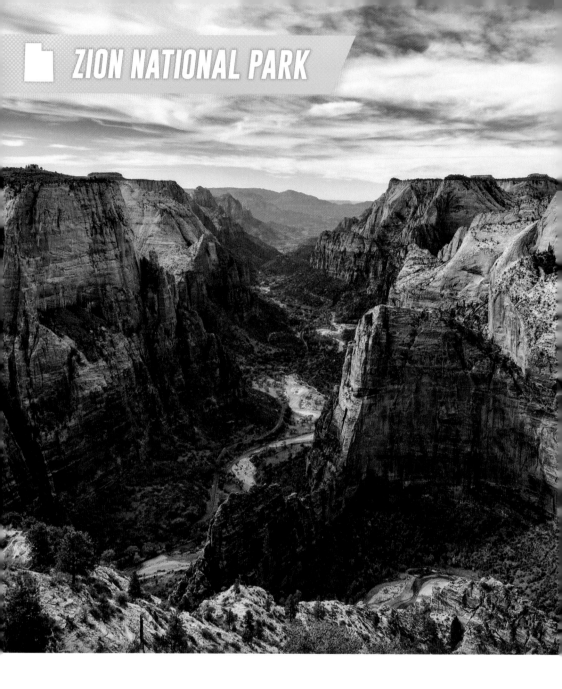

ZION NATIONAL PARK

Two hikers start down a dusty trail in Zion National Park. They have a long, difficult hike ahead of them. The trail zigzags back and forth up the steep rock walls. After some time, it flattens. The hikers enter a shaded **canyon**. Towering walls rise on all sides.

ARCHES NATIONAL PARK

GREAT SALT LAKE

TEMPLE SQUARE

UTAH OLYMPIC PARK

OBSERVATION POINT
ZION NATIONAL PARK

A few hours later, the hikers reach Observation Point. Zion Canyon spreads out before them. They are high above the canyon floor. Long ago, water carved this deep canyon and exposed layers of colorful rock. The hikers enjoy the stunning view. Welcome to Utah!

WHERE IS UTAH?

Utah is located in the western United States. It spreads across 84,897 square miles (219,882 square kilometers). Utah shares its northern border with Idaho. It touches Wyoming in the northeast. Colorado sits to Utah's east. Utah's southern border touches Arizona. Nevada lies to the west.

The state's capital and largest city is Salt Lake City in north-central Utah. It lies in the Wasatch Front. This **metropolitan** area stretches for 105 miles (169 kilometers) along the Wasatch Range. Most of Utah's other major cities, like Provo and Ogden, are also in this region.

NEVADA

ST. GEORGE

IDAHO

WYOMING

● OGDEN

★ SALT LAKE CITY

SANDY

OREM — PROVO

UTAH

COLORADO —

FOUR CORNERS

Utah's southeastern corner touches the corners of Colorado, New Mexico, and Arizona. Where they meet is called the Four Corners. It is the only place in the U.S. where four states meet!

NEW MEXICO

ARIZONA

UTAH'S BEGINNINGS

UTE INDIAN ART

People have lived in Utah for more than 12,000 years. About 1,800 years ago, **Ancestral** Puebloans **settled** the Colorado **Plateau**. They built cliff dwellings for shelter. Later, the Ute, Paiute, and Shoshone tribes settled Utah's lands.

NAMING UTAH

Mormon settlers wanted to name the area Deseret, meaning "honeybee." But in 1850, the United States named the region "Utah." The name comes from the Ute tribe.

Europeans first explored southern Utah in 1765. Fur traders moved through the north in the early 1800s. **Immigrants** traveling to Oregon and California also passed through Utah. In 1847, **Mormon** leader Brigham Young settled the Salt Lake Valley with a group of **pioneers** looking for religious freedom. Their community quickly grew. In 1848, the U.S. gained control of Utah from Mexico. Utah became the 45th state in 1896.

NATIVE PEOPLES OF UTAH

GOSHUTE

- Original lands in the Great Basin area
- Around 530 in Utah today
- Also called Kusiutta

NORTHWESTERN BAND OF THE SHOSHONE NATION

- Original lands in northeastern Utah
- Around 430 in Utah and Idaho today
- Also called Newe

NAVAJO NATION

- Original lands in the Four Corners area
- Around 173,000 in Navajo Nation today
- Also called Diné

UTE

- Original lands around the Great Basin and the Colorado Plateau
- About 2,970 in Utah today
- Also called Nuche

PAIUTE

- Original lands in the Great Basin and the Colorado Plateau
- Around 920 in Utah today

Three major regions make up Utah. In the northeast are the Uinta and Wasatch Ranges of the Rocky Mountains. The dry **Great Basin** stretches across western Utah. The Great Salt Lake and Great Salt Lake Desert are found there. The Colorado Plateau covers eastern and southern Utah. Canyons and valleys carve through this high, desert landscape.

GREAT SALT LAKE

WASATCH RANGE
COLORADO PLATEAU
GREAT BASIN

N
W + E
S

GREAT SALT LAKE

The Great Salt Lake is the largest natural lake in the western United States. It is saltier than the ocean. All that salt makes it easy for swimmers to float!

GREAT SALT LAKE

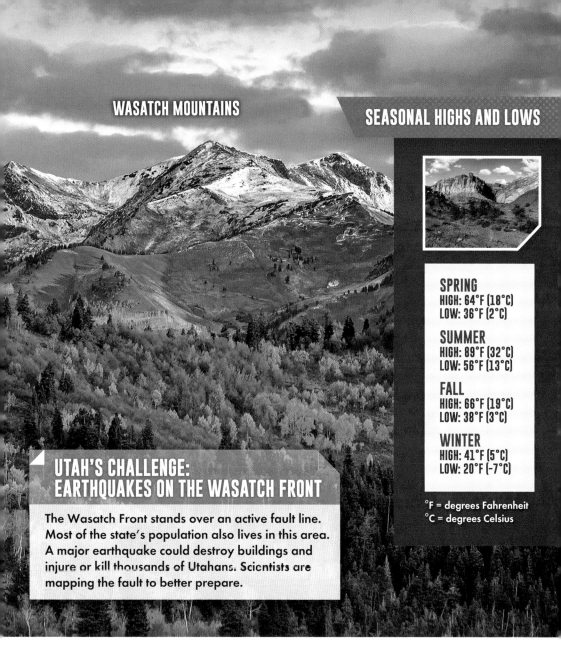

SEASONAL HIGHS AND LOWS

SPRING
HIGH: 64°F (18°C)
LOW: 36°F (2°C)

SUMMER
HIGH: 89°F (32°C)
LOW: 56°F (13°C)

FALL
HIGH: 66°F (19°C)
LOW: 38°F (3°C)

WINTER
HIGH: 41°F (5°C)
LOW: 20°F (-7°C)

°F = degrees Fahrenheit
°C = degrees Celsius

UTAH'S CHALLENGE: EARTHQUAKES ON THE WASATCH FRONT

The Wasatch Front stands over an active fault line. Most of the state's population also lives in this area. A major earthquake could destroy buildings and injure or kill thousands of Utahans. Scientists are mapping the fault to better prepare.

Utah's hot summers follow cold winters. It is among the driest states. Some desert areas see less than 5 inches (13 centimeters) of **precipitation** each year. But some mountain areas receive 40 feet (12 meters) or more of winter snowfall!

11

Hundreds of animal species live in Utah. Rocky Mountain elk, the state animal, graze in the mountains. Mountain goats cross steep land to escape mountain lions and other predators. On the Colorado Plateau, Utah prairie dogs keep watch for hungry hawks and rattlesnakes. **Burrows** protect desert tortoises from the hot sun and coyotes on the hunt.

Each year, seasonal **migration** brings 7.5 million birds to the Great Salt Lake. For a short time, its shores become homes for eared grebes, phalaropes, and white pelicans. Pronghorn and bobcats roam the lake's Antelope Island. A herd of around 600 bison also lives there!

EARED GREBE

GREAT BASIN RATTLESNAKE

MOJAVE DESERT TORTOISE

WHITE PELICAN

RED-TAILED HAWK

ROCKY MOUNTAIN ELK

Life Span: 8 to 12 years
Status: least concern

Rocky Mountain elk range = ▬

LEAST CONCERN	NEAR THREATENED	VULNERABLE	ENDANGERED	CRITICALLY ENDANGERED	EXTINCT IN THE WILD	EXTINCT

More than 3.2 million people call Utah home. Four out of five live in and around the cities of the Wasatch Front. Many of Utah's Native Americans live on **reservations**. The Navajo, Ute, and Paiute are among Utah's five Native American tribes.

UTAH'S CHALLENGE: AIR POLLUTION

The Wasatch Front often faces poor air quality. In the winter, warm air may trap cooler air below it. Car use and other human activities pollute this lower air. As a result, the air can become unhealthy to breathe.

Almost 4 out of 5 Utahans have European ancestry. Hispanic Americans make up the next-largest group. Utah also has smaller populations of Black or African Americans, Asian Americans, and Pacific Islanders. Native Americans make up about 1 out of 100 Utahans. Immigrants living in Utah often arrived from Mexico, Peru, Venezuela, or India.

Salt Lake City stands between the Great Salt Lake and the Wasatch Range. The Ute and Shoshone people once lived in the area. Mormon pioneers founded the city in 1847. In 1849, gold-seekers passed through on their way to California. They boosted the young city's population. Salt Lake City became the capital of the Utah **Territory** in 1856.

Today, **tourism** keeps Salt Lake City busy. The city draws Mormons from around the world. They visit the Salt Lake Temple, Tabernacle, and other religious sites. Other tourists come for the nearby ski areas. In 2002, the city hosted thousands of visitors for the Winter Olympics!

2002 WINTER OLYMPICS IN SALT LAKE CITY

A WORLD CAPITAL

More than half of Utahans are Mormon. They belong to the Church of Jesus Christ of Latter-day Saints. The religion's world capital is based in Salt Lake City!

SALT LAKE TEMPLE

17

INDUSTRY

PARK RANGER

Three out of four Utahans work in the **service industry**. They may have jobs in real estate, government, or banks. The state's national parks and beautiful scenery make tourism a major industry. Many Utahans support tourists at ski resorts, wilderness areas, and hotels. Farming is also important. Milk, beef, and hay are among the state's top farm products.

HAY FIELD

Utah is rich with **natural resources**. Miners dig gold, silver, copper, and minerals from the earth. Coal and oil come from the Colorado Plateau. Utahans **manufacture** transportation equipment, electronics, computers, and food products.

INVENTED IN UTAH

ARTIFICIAL HEART
Date Invented: 1982
Inventors: Willem Johan Kolff, Robert Jarvik, and University of Utah team

ELECTRIC TRAFFIC LIGHT
Date Invented: 1912
Inventor: Lester Wire

FRY SAUCE
Date Invented: 1940s
Inventor: Don Carlos Edwards

NAVAJO TACO

Utahans like a wide range of foods. Many restaurants serve pastrami burgers. These sandwiches have a hamburger patty with a hearty stack of pastrami on top! Utahans also enjoy Navajo tacos. This dish uses **fry bread** as a base for meat, vegetables, salsa, and beans. Funeral potatoes is another popular dish. It is a cheesy potato casserole topped with crunchy cornflakes.

FUNERAL POTATOES

Utah's summers bring tasty fresh produce. Utahans enjoy Bear Lake raspberries fresh or mixed in a milkshake. Green River's famously sweet watermelons, cantaloupes, and other melons are another summer treat. Utahans may also put fresh fruit in Jell-O, the state snack.

RASPBERRY MILKSHAKE

FRY SAUCE

MAKES ABOUT 1 1/4 CUPS

Salt Lake City is the birthplace of this popular Utah condiment. People enjoy similar sauces around the world, such as Argentina's *salsa golf.*

INGREDIENTS

1 cup mayonnaise

1/4 cup ketchup

1/2 tablespoon dill pickle juice

1/2 teaspoon Worcestershire sauce

1/8 teaspoon salt

1/8 teaspoon paprika

pinch of cayenne pepper

DIRECTIONS

1. Combine all of the ingredients in a bowl.

2. Whisk the ingredients together until they are fully combined.

3. Refrigerate to let the flavors mix together.

4. Start dipping! Fry sauce tastes great with french fries, salads, and hamburgers.

CANYONEERING

Five national parks and forty-four state parks make Utah great for outdoor lovers. Utahans enjoy hiking, rock climbing, boating, and **canyoneering** in these wilderness areas. Snowy mountain resorts draw skiers and snowboarders. Each summer, professional bicyclists crisscross the state in the week-long Tour of Utah race.

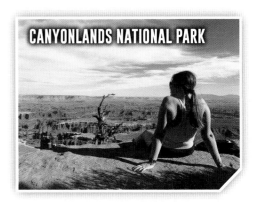

CANYONLANDS NATIONAL PARK

22

Utahans love to cheer for their state's professional basketball and soccer teams. Many also follow sports teams at local universities. Utahans are music lovers, too. Many attend live concerts of the famous Tabernacle Choir. Symphonies, operas, and dance performances are also popular.

BONNEVILLE SPEEDWAY

The wide-open Bonneville Salt Flats make a natural setting for racing. Each year, the famous Bonneville Speedway puts on popular car and motorcycle races. Many speed records have been broken there!

NOTABLE SPORTS TEAM

Real Salt Lake
Sport: Major League Soccer
Started: 2004
Place of Play: Rio Tinto Stadium

Festivals bring Utahans together. Each spring, Ute around the state hold their yearly Bear Dance. Their singing, drumming, and dancing celebrate being alive. On July 24, statewide Pioneer Day events mark Brigham Young's arrival to the Salt Lake Valley. Utahans honor the state's early settlers with concerts, rodeos, fireworks, and colorful parades.

September's Peach Days festival comes with the fall harvest in Brigham City. Visitors sample peach cobbler, deep-fried peaches, and other peach dishes. From June to October, Cedar City hosts the Utah Shakespeare Festival. This popular theater festival gives Utahans the chance to celebrate their love of the arts!

UTAH SHAKESPEARE FESTIVAL

SUNDANCE FILM FESTIVAL

Every winter, Park City hosts the famous Sundance Film Festival. Thousands of celebrities and movie-lovers come to watch new independent films. Utahan actor and director Robert Redford's Sundance Institute has run the festival since 1985!

SUNDANCE FILM FESTIVAL

1847

Brigham Young and a group of Mormon pioneers establish Salt Lake City

1881

The U.S. government begins pushing the Ute people onto the Uintah and Ouray reservations

AROUND 1300

Ancestral Puebloans leave the Colorado Plateau

1765

The first Europeans arrive in Utah

1869

The final spike of the first transcontinental railroad is driven into track laid at Promontory, Utah

1896

Utah becomes the 45th
state on January 4

2002

Salt Lake City hosts
the Winter Olympics

2009

Reul Salt Lake wins
the MLS Cup

1929

Arches National Park
is established

Nickname: The Beehive State

Motto: Industry

Date of Statehood: January 4, 1896 (the 45th state)

Capital City: Salt Lake City ★

Other Major Cities: Provo, West Jordan, Orem, Sandy, Ogden, St. George

Area: 84,897 square miles (219,882 square kilometers);
Utah is the 13th largest state.

Population

3,271,616 (2020)

STATE FLAG

Adopted in 2011, Utah's flag features a dark blue background. At its center is the state seal. The state seal includes two crossed American flags, a bald eagle, and a shield. On the shield, there is a beehive to stand for Utah's state nickname, the Beehive State. It is surrounded by sego lilies, the state flower. The flowers stand for peace. The state's motto, "Industry," appears above the beehive. The state's name is below the beehive. The dates 1847 and 1896 refer to the year Mormons settled Utah and the year Utah became a state.

INDUSTRY

JOBS

- MANUFACTURING **7%**
- FARMING AND NATURAL RESOURCES **2%**
- GOVERNMENT **14%**
- SERVICES **77%**

Main Exports

computers

medical products

chemicals

transportation equipment

electronics

food products

Natural Resources
coal, petroleum, natural gas, gold, silver, copper, oil shale, tar sands, beryllium

GOVERNMENT

Federal Government
4 REPRESENTATIVES | **2** SENATORS

6 ELECTORAL VOTES

USA

UT

State Government
75 REPRESENTATIVES | **29** SENATORS

STATE SYMBOLS

STATE BIRD
CALIFORNIA GULL

STATE ANIMAL
ROCKY MOUNTAIN ELK

STATE FLOWER
SEGO LILY

STATE TREE
QUAKING ASPEN

GLOSSARY

ancestral—related to relatives who lived long ago

burrows—holes animals make in the ground

canyon—a deep and narrow valley that has steep sides

canyoneering—exploring a canyon by means such as hiking, swimming, rafting, or climbing

fry bread—a Native American flatbread made from frying dough

Great Basin—a broad, dry region in the western United States that does not drain to an ocean

immigrants—people who move to a new country

manufacture—to make products, often with machines

metropolitan—the combined city and suburban area

migration—the act of traveling from one place to another, often with the seasons

Mormon—related to the Church of Jesus Christ of Latter-day Saints

natural resources—materials in the earth that are taken out and used to make products or fuel

pioneers—people who are among the first to explore or settle in an area

plateau—an area of flat, raised land

precipitation—water that falls to the earth as rain, snow, sleet, mist, or hail

reservations—areas of land that are controlled by Native American tribes

service industry—a group of businesses that perform tasks for people or other businesses

settled—moved somewhere and made it home

territory—an area of land under the control of a government; territories in the United States are considered part of the country but do not have power in the government.

tourism—the business of people traveling to visit other places

AT THE LIBRARY

Goddu, Krystyna Poray. *Native Peoples of the Great Basin.* Minneapolis, Minn.: Lerner Publications, 2017.

Hamilton, John. *Utah: The Beehive State.* Minneapolis, Minn.: Abdo Publishing, 2017.

McHugh, Erin. *National Parks: A Kid's Guide to America's Parks, Monuments, and Landmarks.* New York, N.Y.: Black Dog & Leventhal Publishers, 2019.

ON THE WEB

FACTSURFER

Factsurfer.com gives you a safe, fun way to find more information.

1. Go to www.factsurfer.com.

2. Enter "Utah" into the search box and click 🔍.

3. Select your book cover to see a list of related content.

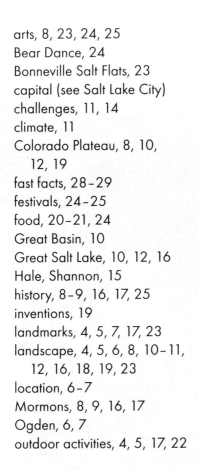

INDEX

HOWELL

Beginner's Guide to

Aquariums

John Coborn

Editor
Dennis Kelsey-Wood

HOWELL BOOK HOUSE Inc.
230 Park Avenue
New York, N.Y. 10169

Library of Congress Cataloging-in-Publication Data

Coborn, John.
  Howell beginner's guide to aquariums.

  Summary: Discusses the basic aspects of establishing an aquarium in the home and developing it into a successful miniature ecosystem, including equipment, maintenance, and the requirements of coldwater, tropical, and marine aquariums.
    1. Aquariums. (1. Aquariums) I. Kelsey-Wood, Dennis. II. Title. III. Title: Beginner's guide to aquariums.
SF457.C58 1986   639.3'4   86-20025
ISBN 0-87605-900-0

Photographic credits:

© Ray Parry: pp. 11, 30 (top)
© Ric Fallu: pp. 31 (top), 42 (bottom)
© Brian Hay: pp. 43 (bottom)
© Positive Image Photographic Library: pp. 43 (top)
© Paradise Press: All others and illustrations.

Printed in Australia by Fast Proof Press Pty. Ltd.

Contents

Introduction

The origins of aquarium keeping are steeped in history, but there is evidence that the Chinese were the first to keep fish alive in indoor containers for recreational and aesthetic purposes. The common goldfish, which originated in the Far East, was probably the first species to be cultivated on a large scale, initially as a food item for the dinner tables of Chinese aristocracy. It was not long before varieties of colour and shape persuaded pioneer aquarists to proudly display their latest acquisitions in elaborately carved, stone receptacles, which fitted in with the exquisite interior design of that period. All this took place as far back as the tenth century, and it is from these early beginnings that the science — and a science it is indeed — of fishkeeping has developed to the advanced stage it has reached today. The first goldfish arrived in Europe, via Japan, probably in the seventeenth century and by the early nineteen hundreds, the fancy was already at an advanced stage in most parts of the civilized world.

The Oranda goldfish

It was not long before other fish species drew the attention of early aquarists, and the delight of seeing those little gems known collectively as tropical fish, for the first time, must have been exhilarating. In the early days, of course, a huge percentage of those fish captured in the wild and exported to alien climes, perished in transit or shortly after arrival, and it has taken many years of research by dedicated enthusiasts to arrive at the much happier situation we have today. Modern methods of breeding and transport mean that a huge variety of species is available to the average aquarist, and the many sophisticated appliances on the market mean that most species can thrive in the captive environment which has been designed, as closely as possible, to resemble the original wild habitat. In recent times, the manufacturers of aquarists' equipment have taken the trouble to send qualified scientists to areas where various species are native, to make detailed studies of the biotope. This has further increased what was a somewhat skimpy knowledge of the conditions necessary to create an ecologically correct portion of nature in the home.

The lower vertebrates, including fish, amphibia and reptiles, are unable to adapt to alien environments in the same way that mammals and birds do. The only answer, therefore, is to provide as closely as possible, a facsimile of the environment to which they are already adapted. Once the correct balance has been achieved, we are rewarded not only with happy, healthy fish and luxuriant plant growth, but also the joy of seeing our charges, behaving and reproducing in much the same way as they would in some distant jungle stream.

Marine fishkeeping is a relative newcomer to the hobby and, again, it has taken many years of collective research to reach the situation where marine fish can live a natural lifespan in a captive situation. Tropical coral reef fish are the most popular, due to their impressive coloration and variety, and it is now possible to keep a whole section of a coral reef, complete with all its life forms, in a moderately sized tank within the home. Our knowledge of the biology of many marine animals is still somewhat sparse when compared with freshwater specimens, and few species of coral fish are regularly bred in captivity. However, with the dedicated research constantly applied by both amateur and professional marine biologists, it will not be long before the trapping of wild specimens for the aquarist will be a thing of the past.

It can be seen, that the prospective aquarist has a wide choice of subjects on which to concentrate his efforts, and there is a huge range of aquariums and equipment on the market to tempt the beginner. It is recommended that anyone embarking on the hobby of aquarium keeping, should first start off with a simple cold water tank, containing maybe a few goldfish and thus acquiring that initial 'feel' before embarking on a more ambitious project. There are, of course, those who so enjoy the goldfish varieties, that they have no compulsion to venture into the intricacies of tropical or marine aquaristics, but the natural progression it would seem is from cold water, to tropical, to marine and any one can remain at any point which appeals the most, on the way.

It is the object of this small volume, to briefly introduce each of the different kinds of aquarium keeping, to point out the advantages and disadvantages of each, and to help the beginner decide what is going to be the appropriate course of action. Space does not permit a comprehensive study of any branch of the hobby and the enthusiast is refered to other books specializing in the individual subjects. However, the author hopes to cover all those salient points which will arise in the initial stages and guide the novice into the fascinating world of aquarium keeping. All measurements in the book use the metric system but a useful conversion table will be found at the end of the text.

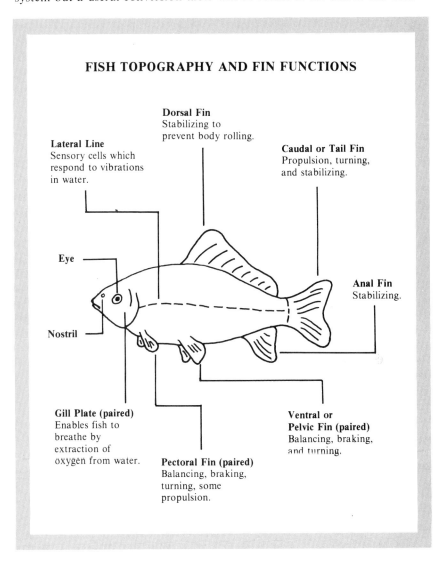

FISH TOPOGRAPHY AND FIN FUNCTIONS

Dorsal Fin
Stabilizing to prevent body rolling.

Lateral Line
Sensory cells which respond to vibrations in water.

Caudal or Tail Fin
Propulsion, turning, and stabilizing.

Eye

Anal Fin
Stabilizing.

Nostril

Gill Plate (paired)
Enables fish to breathe by extraction of oxygen from water.

Pectoral Fin (paired)
Balancing, braking, turning, some propulsion.

Ventral or Pelvic Fin (paired)
Balancing, braking, and turning.

1. Aquariums and Equipment

Whatever kind of underwater environment one wishes to reproduce, the basic aquarium will be similar. There are, of course, certain aspects to be borne in mind with each of the different branches of fishkeeping, but these will be dealt with in the appropriate chapters. There are several kinds of aquarium available and a few of the more usual types are discussed here.

The Plastic Aquarium

Perhaps the cheapest and most readily available type of aquarium is that manufactured from transparent plastic. Such tanks are usually cast in a single mold and attractively shaped with the sides sloping outwards from the base, which may be decorated with a frame in an opaque color. A colored aquarium cover is usually supplied with the tank and this may contain various brackets for lighting and other equipment. Plastic tanks come in various sizes, ranging from about five litre capacity and upwards. For the beginner, with a small budget, the plastic tank is ideal for initiation. The synthetic materials from which the tanks are manufactured are inert and will not be affected by the chemical compounds contained in the various aquarium waters. Another advantage is that they are light-weight, easy to transport and may be stacked to store away in a minimum amount of space. The only major disadvantage they seem to have is that the plastic surfaces become covered with a mist of minute scratches after regular cleaning, which affects the crystal clarity of the view into the aquascene. However, with the continuing advancement in the production of synthetic materials, it may not be long before we have a tank which will stand up to the same rigors as glass. Plastic tanks are always useful to keep as quarantine, hospital or stock containers, even to those aquarists who have advanced to glass display tanks.

Molded Glass Tanks

Similar to the molded plastic tanks, but made from glass in a single cast, these tanks are useful as stock, or small standby containers. They are usually unsuitable as display tanks as they rarely come in sizes greater than sixty litre capacity and the method of manufacture results in irregularities in the thickness of the glass, which will create a distorted view of the contents.

Framed Tanks

Tanks consisting of glass sheets in a frame of various materials have been very popular in the recent past. The main material for the framework in the original tanks of this type was iron or steel, and the glass was held in with ordinary glazing putty. The disadvantages of this were that the metal would soon corrode, due to the close proximity to water and the continual oxygenation. Not only was the framework soon weakened, but the iron oxides released from the metal would pollute the water to levels dangerous to the fish. These tanks could not be stored for long in a dry condition without the putty cracking and resulting in leaks as soon as the tank was refilled. Various improvements on these framed tanks were gradually developed over the years. The frames were initially painted to delay the corrosion of the metal but the composition of the paint itself was often of a dubious nature. Soon, plastic coating of the frames became the norm, but there always seemed to be spots where moisture could penetrate through the plastic and set off a corrosive reaction on the metal, which would result in the plastic peeling away. New kinds of putty were developed which would not dry out and remained elastic, the weight of the water itself, in the tank, would form a seal against the elastic layer and prevent leaks.

Swordtails in a well-planted aquarium.

Aluminum and alloy frames of various composition were tried out but the problem of corrosion remained, particularly with regard to salt water aquariums. By far the best type of framed tanks to date are those consisting of stainless steel, the glass being held in place by elastic putty. The frames are attractive in appearance as well as being relatively corrosion free, although even stainless steel is not recommended for marine tanks.

Recent experiments with plastic framed tanks have not proven too popular. There is a limit to the size of such tanks as the pressure of water in a large capacity container would soon bow a frame which was insufficiently rigid. Small versions of such tanks are, however, suitable for fry rearing, hospital, or quarantine for small numbers of fish.

All Glass Tanks

The advent of silicon rubber bonding and sealing compounds has revolutionized the construction of the home aquarium, and it is now possible for almost any one to construct a tank with little more than five sheets of glass of the required size, and a couple of tubes of aquarium sealer. Many aquarists' suppliers will of course supply such tanks ready made, or will make them to the specifications of the buyer who has not the time or the inclination to make his own. All glass tanks have many distinct advantages over all other types. They are corrosion free and lack the problems associated with leaking frames, the panes will not scratch, as will plastic, and they can be made to look extremely attractive with the minimum amount of expense.

To construct a tank of say 60 cm long x 30 cm wide x 30 cm deep the following sized sheets of 5mm thick plate glass are required:

1 base	60 cm x 30 cm
1 front	60 cm x 30 cm
1 back	60 cm x 30 cm
2 ends	30 cm x 35 cm
Including allowance for glass thickness	

Your local glass merchant will be pleased to cut the panes to size and mill off any sharp edges; it is advisable to have the edges which will form the top of the tank milled to prevent accidents during routine maintenance.

Having obtained the glass and sufficient silicon rubber bonding material for the tank required, lay the base plate on a firm, flat surface, preferably covered with an old blanket or several thicknesses of newspaper. Squeeze a thin layer of bonding material (to the manufacturer's recommendations) along the upper surface of the edge on one of the long sides. Take the back panel and embed it into the silicon layer, holding it in position with one hand whilst applying bonding material to the edge of one of the ends. It is possible to carry out this operation by oneself, but somewhat easier if a little help can be solicited. One end panel can be slid into position and held firm by strips of adhesive tape. The whole tank is systematically assembled, using enough adhesive tape to hold the panes in position while the compound is setting. For added strength and insurance against leaks, the inner angles of the tank should be further sealed with a triangular section strip of the bonding material which can be squeezed along the inner joints from a special nozzle. For additional strength, strips of glass about 5 cm wide can be cemented along the top edges of the tank. Silicon rubber compound can be smoothed into place, using a wet finger, before it is set. After setting, which usually takes not more than a couple of hours, excess sealer can be scraped away with a razor blade. To be absolutely safe, it is advisable to leave the adhesive tape in position for about twelve hours, or overnight, before removing it.

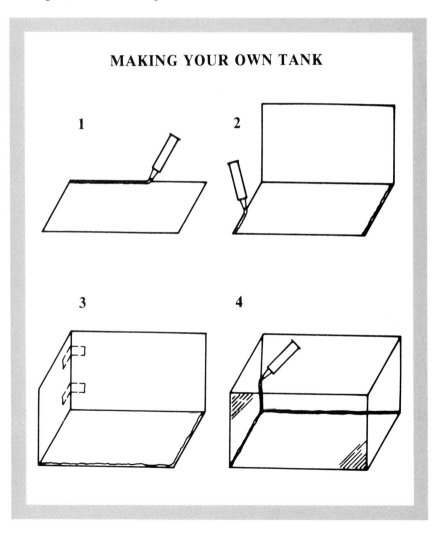

MAKING YOUR OWN TANK

Capacity

There is a strong connection between tank capacities and the number of fish which can be comfortably kept. Water only contains a given amount of oxygen at any one time, and if this oxygen is used up by fish in respiration without being replaced, they will soon suffocate. The most important measurement in an aquarium is the surface area, which will dictate the number of fish which can be safely kept. In a tank which is not receiving mechanical aeration, we can safely keep 5 cm of fish length (not including the tail) to each 300 square centimetres of surface area, so that, in our tank with a water surface area of 60 cm x 30 cm (1800 sq cm), we can keep 30 cm of fish length. This, of course, can consist of ten fish of three centimetres length, six fish of five centimetres length, or any combination of lengths, providing the total does not exceed 30 cm when fully grown.

In a tank receiving mechanical aeration, the total length of fish can be increased. Using a different formula, the capacity of the tank in litres is first calculated, which in our example will be 60 cm x 30 cm x 30 cm equalling 54000 cu cm. As there are 1000 cu cm to the litre, it can be seen that the tank capacity is 54 litres. We can allow 1cm of fish length to each litre of water, thus being able to accommodate 27 fish of two centimetres length, eighteen of three centimetres length, or any other combination providing the total does not exceed 54 cms. These measurements are given as guidelines only, as many other factors will contribute towards the number of fish which can be kept in a given volume, including aeration capacity, temperature, water movement, numbers of plants and species of fish. With experience, the aquarist will know at what point to stop before incurring any unnecessary risks.

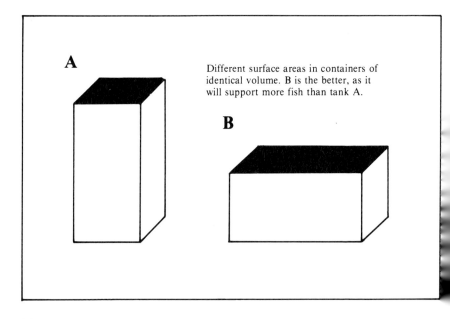

A

Different surface areas in containers of identical volume. B is the better, as it will support more fish than tank A.

B

Heating

Supplementary heating is required for tropical and marine aquaria; cold water aquaria do not require any heating, unless they are kept in outhouses in cold climates. In some cases, certain temperate marine tanks may even require cooling in the summer months. There are several kinds of aquarium heaters available and, for the tank with a capacity of fifty to one hundred litres, a single 100 watt element, contained in a heat resistant glass tube and controlled by a thermostat, is adequate to maintain the water temperature at the desired level. Different species of fish are, of course, most comfortable in the temperatures which are optimum in their natural habitats, and certain taxa from temperate climates may require some seasonal variation. However, the majority of tropical fish which come from equatorial regions, both freshwater and marine, thrive at a temperature range of 24°-28° C. Glass tube heaters should be placed near the base of the tank, so that the heated water will rise and create convection currents which will spread the temperature equally about the tank. Thermostats may be incorporated with the heating tube or may be separate and can be set to the required temperature.

Recent research has shown that the temperature of moving water in tropical climates remains fairly constant day and night as well as throughout the year; in addition, vertical and horizontal water movement ensures equal distribution of heat from substrate to surface. Thermostatically controlled heating cables, which can be placed in the substrate gravel of the aquarium, are a relatively new innovation, producing constant temperatures throughout the tank. Such heaters are of particular value to aquatic plants which, with the use of more conventional heaters, would be denied adequate heat at root level. Convection through the substrate is also an excellent method of dispersing organic wastes and detritus into the main body of water, where it can more easily be removed by filtration.

An essential part of every aquarist's equipment is a reliable thermometer. Various kinds are available ranging from a floating type to one which is fixed to the side of the tank with a suction bracket. Temperatures should be monitored regularly to ensure that the heating system is functioning correctly. It is now possible to obtain an electronic thermometer with a digital reading which can be easily observed outside the tank.

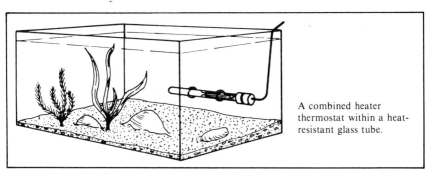

A combined heater thermostat within a heat-resistant glass tube.

Lighting

Adequate lighting is of utmost importance where aquatic plants are to thrive. A particularly essential part of green plant biology known as photosynthesis can only function under certain light intensities. The process consists of the absorption of carbon dioxide gas from the water (or from the air in terrestrial conditions) through the foliage. The gas is combined with water to produce organic building materials, using chlorophyll and sunlight as a catalyst. Most fish species also, can only live a natural life if supplied with a light/dark cycle similar to that found in the natural habitat. In tropical regions the light/dark cycle is almost equal, with seasonal variations increasing as one gets further from the equator. Most tropical fish (and plants) therefore require about twelve hours of light and twelve hours of darkness in each twenty four hour day.

Quality of light is as important as intensity and the days of using a couple of domestic light bulbs over the aquarium are over; that is, if one requires to strike a healthy community balance. Modern research has produced a number of makes of broad spectrum fluorescent tubes which produce light of a quality almost the same as natural sunlight. Two such tubes of 20 watts mounted in a special hood about 70 cm in length will be adequate for a tank with around 100 litre capacity. The greater the capacity of the tank the higher the wattage required as is indicated in the following table.

Aquarium Capacity (in litres)	Number and Strength of Lamps
60	1 x 30 watts
100	2 x 20 Watts
150	2 x 30 Watts
200	2 x 40 Watts
250	3 x 40 Watts
400	3 x 60 Watts

The special hoods which are supplied to house these lamps are usually made from attractive materials and are lined with reflective material to give maximum output from the lights into the water. For very large capacity tanks, high intensity, mercury vapor lamps are available which can be used in conjunction with the fluorescent tubes. Due to the amount of heat emitted by such lights, they should be mounted at least thirty centimetres above the water surface, from where they will brilliantly illuminate chosen parts of the aquarium contents.

Aeration

In theory, a well planted tank should not require additional aeration as photosynthesis should produce adequate oxygen to supply the animal forms. In practice, however, there are many factors which affect the correct functioning of plants in the tank and the addition of mechanical aeration will supplement any inadequacies. Air pumps come in various sizes and may consist of a simple electrically operated diaphragm type suitable for the single tank, ranging up to the more sophisticated piston type pumps of a size sufficient to aerate several aquaria. For the aquarist with a large number of tanks it may pay to purchase a small compressor which will ensure a permanent air supply.

Air from the pump, whatever the type, is conveyed to the tank by a narrow plastic tube at the end of which is placed a diffuser stone. As air is forced through the stone it is split up into a stream of bubbles which rises to the water surface. This process not only causes air to be absorbed from the bubbles themselves, but creates currents which ensure that all of the water in the tank reaches the surface at some stage, allowing further gas exchange. It is best to position the air diffuser somewhere near the bottom of the tank to allow maximum effect. Various clamps are available to regulate air supply and with more sophisticated equipment, a reducing valve may be used. With the use of 'T' joints, several tanks can be supplied from a single aerator, providing it is of adequate capacity.

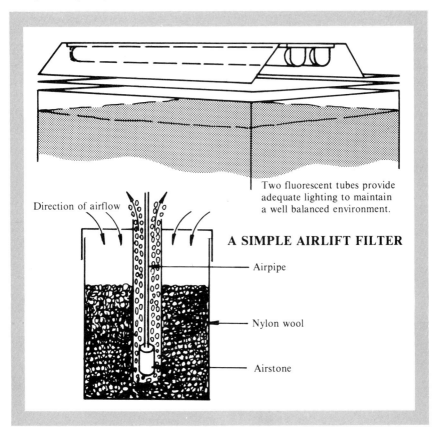

Direction of airflow

Two fluorescent tubes provide adequate lighting to maintain a well balanced environment.

A SIMPLE AIRLIFT FILTER

Airpipe

Nylon wool

Airstone

Filtration

Another important addition to the aquarium is an efficient filtration system. For the average home tank, a simple air-lift filter may be used. This consists of a box or cylinder, usually made from clear or tinted plastic, which is loosely packed with a filter medium such as nylon wool. The air diffuser stone is placed in a central tube in the container and the rising air bubbles create a current which pulls the water through the filter medium and removes suspended particles, maintaining a crystal clarity in the water. For larger tanks, power filters are available which are mounted outside the tank, preferably in a concealed position. A powerful pump takes water from the tank, forces it through a filter medium and returns the treated water. Often, such filters will perform additional functions; for instance a layer of peat, or charcoal in the filter medium will help sweeten the water or adjust acidity.

Another kind of filter is that known as a biological gravity filter. This consists of a simple container mounted above the tank, filled with biological chips. These may consist of smooth pebbles, glass marbles or specially manufactured, inert plastic chips. The water is pumped out of the tank, either mechanically or by air-lift and allowed to percolate through the filter, from whence it will return to the aquarium by gravity. After a few weeks the biological chips in the filter will develop a slimy coat, consisting of bacterial colonies which will continually work on the passing water, converting potentially dangerous waste materials into harmless plant nutrients. Such a biological filter is of particular value when used in conjunction with a marine tank.

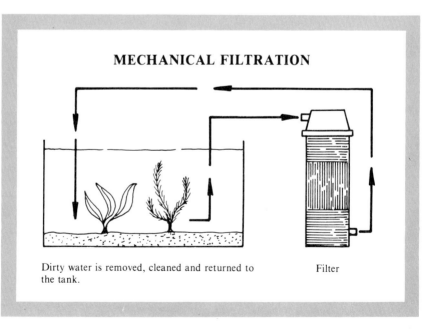

MECHANICAL FILTRATION

Dirty water is removed, cleaned and returned to the tank.

Filter

2. Setting Up the Aquarium

Having decided on the type of aquarium one wishes to keep and obtained the necessary basic equipment, the next stage is to set up the tank in the position it is to permanently occupy. Aquariums, preferably should not be placed in front of a window as the light source will create problems with the plants and possibly the fish, bearing in mind that wild habitats receive light from the top only. Another consideration is whether the aquarium base or stand is used, it is capable of withstanding the not inconsiderable weight of a fish tank containing rocks, gravel and water; a collapsing stand is not one of the happier moments in the aquarist's career! Before putting the tank in position, it is advisable to place a sheet of expanded polystyrene about one centimetre in thickness on the surface of the stand to aid stability as the tank is being filled. Failing this, several thicknesses of corrugated cardboard or newspaper may be used.

Ensure that the interior of the tank is spotlessly clean before proceeding and it is a good idea to test for leaks, by filling with water and waiting for a couple of hours. Any leaks may be quickly repaired using silicon sealer while the tank is empty.

A well set up marine tank. The marine aquarium requires more regular attention than a freshwater aquarium.

Substrate

The substrate is the bottom medium of any stretch of water in which plants grow and small organisms perform a multitude of functions. In the aquarium with its relatively small bottom area, a compromise substrate, which will function as near as possible to the natural habitat conditions, has to be used. For cold and tropical freshwater aquaria, the basic ingredient for the substrate is graded gravel or shingle; exceptionally, artificial gravel available in various colors may be used. For marine aquaria, the substrate composition is necessarily different and will be dealt with in chapter six.

Washed river sand or shingle is perfectly satisfactory but it is advisable to sterilize it before use. First pass a jet of cold water through it and swill it about to remove fine particles and dust, then boil it in a metal container for about fifteen minutes. It is then further swilled with cold water and drained ready for use. Even commercially bought gravel should be washed before use, to remove any dust which may have accumulated during storage. The gravel is laid in the bottom of the aquarium, sloping from the front towards the back. Not only does this look better, but uneaten fish food and sediment will work its way into the trough at the front of the tank, rendering it easier to remove. In a tank of say 30 cm breadth, a slope 3 cm deep at the front graded up to 8 cm at the back will be adequate.

For some plants, it is necessary to place various additives below the gravel to provide a nutritious growing medium. Various commercial additives are available which are manufactured to resemble the kind of substrate found in tropical waters. A good compromise is a mixture of one part sterilized garden loam to one part peat. A layer of this about 5 mm thick should be placed about 2 cm below the gravel surface.

Rocks and Decorations

Rocks in the aquarium add that touch of authenticity, and artistic layout can create valleys, terraces and caves. Select rocks with care, only using those which are inert and unlikely to release chemical compounds into the water. In general, limestone should be avoided but sandstone, granite, flint and even washed coal are suitable. Rocks should be bedded securely in the substrate and those with strata should preferably follow a natural line. Some dealers supply artificial rocks made from various materials. These are usually safe to use and are often most attractive.

Other decorative materials include unusually shaped pieces of wood. Special bogwood is available from dealers, and this has usually been treated to render it inert. If collecting your own wood, such as tree roots or bits of tree branches, ensure that it is dead and that the sap has dried out; some saps can be poisonous to fish. One way of ensuring safety is to boil the wood for several hours, then soak it for several days, changing the water daily. Tree roots in particular can be very attractively arranged in the tank, to resemble the genuine item growing into the water.

Although the author prefers a natural looking tank, some aquarists like to have other decorative materials in their tanks. Such objects as plastic or ceramic mermaids, galleons and treasure chests, and even Mickey Mouses which blow bubbles out of their mouths at regular intervals, are available.

Planting

Living plants are a most important aspect of both cold and tropical freshwater aquaria. Not only do green plants absorb carbon dioxide from the water and give out oxygen in exchange, they perform the function of filters and cleaners, absorbing waste animal products and converting them into harmless substances. There are as many different types of plant available to the aquarist as there are fish and, like the latter they come from varying habitats and have individual requirements. Some for instance, like hard, alkaline water, whilst others will only survive in soft acid water. When choosing fish and plants therefore, it is important to have only those species which are compatible with similar conditions in the community tank. In addition, it is wise to limit your number of plant species to two or three, otherwise the stronger plants will soon flourish at the expense of the others. Plant thickly with tall growing varieties at the rear of the tank and down the sides; a few short growing species may be planted in the foreground, but be sure to leave an adequate swimming area for the fish.

Most plants are supplied ready rooted or as cuttings. They can be pushed gently into the substance, using a special fork ended planting rod. Some plants may persistently break free from the substrate and float to the surface, particularly cuttings. To prevent this happening, a few ceramic or glass beads may be tied to the plant base with a little nylon thread, before it is inserted into the gravel. At one time, lead wire was recommended to weight the plants but, as with most metals, this could have a detrimental effect on the water composition. Many plant species may require additional nutrients to those immediately available from fish wastes. There are several kinds of excellent plant feeding tablets available on the market, which should be used to the manufacturer's instructions. The tablets are normally inserted into the substrate, near to the roots. Modern technology has produced a system of feeding aquarium plants by regular electronically controlled injections of liquid manure into the water in minute quantities.

Cold Water Plants

Of the many species of aquatic plants suitable for the cold water aquarium, space permits the mention of only a few of the better known varieties. Canadian pond weed, *Elodea canadensis* and the closely related anacharis, *Elodea densa* are two very useful plants which are easy to propagate from cuttings. Both species are prolific and tall growing and regular pruning may be necessary to keep them in check. Tape grass, *Vallisneria spiralis*, with its lush green, ribbon like leaves is another popular plant which makes a good partnership with *Elodea*. It reproduces by runners and little rooted plants are formed at intervals. These may be removed and planted elsewhere. Willow moss, **Fontinalis antipyretica**, is a true moss which anchors itself on submerged stones and roots. In the aquarium, it is best tied to a rock with a little nylon thread until it gets a foothold. Hornwort, **Ceratophyllum demersum**, with its attractive feathery leaves is suited to alkaline waters. Dwarf rush, **Acorus gramineus**, is a short growing species, suitable for the tank foregound.

Elodea densa

Hornwort (*Ceratophyllum demersum*) is suited to Alkaline conditions.

Tropical Plants

The number of tropical aquatic plants available to the aquarist is continually on the increase as the aquarium technology progresses and more difficult species come on the market. Again, it is possible to mention only a few of the more traditional varieties here, but for a more detailed introduction to aquatic plants and their care, the reader is recommended to obtain a companion volume in this series: *'Beginner's Guide to Aquarium Plants and Decoration'*.

Amazon sword genus *Echinodorus* are some of the most popular aquarium plants.

Cabomba aquatica is a very decorative plant, which requires slightly acid water.

Parrot's feather *Myriophyllum braziliense*.

Amazon swords of the genus **Echinodorus** from Central and South America are some of the most popular aquarium plants, with their bright green sword shaped leaves. Long shoots should be trimmed off regularly so that underwater growth is encouraged. Another genus with many species suitable for the aquarium is **Aponogeton**; some have long, slender, erect leaves, whilst others produce narrow, oval shaped leaves, growing at right angles to the stem. One species, known as the Madagascar lace plant, **Aponogeton fenestralis**, has a lattice-work of little windows between the leaf veins.

The genus **Cryptocoryne**, from tropical Asia, contains many interesting species and one of the easiest to grow is **Cryptocoryne affinis**, which has leaves of dark green on the upper surface and wine red beneath. Most species in this genus require soft, slightly acid water. **Hygrophila polysperma**, from India, is an attractive plant with narrow, ovate leaves which will soon form bushy growth if the growing tips are regularly pinched out. **Cabomba aquatica** is a very decorative plant with dark green, opposed leaves, which are divided into feathery segments. Coming from tropical South America, this plant requires soft, slightly acid to neutral water. Water milfoils of the genus **Myriophyllum**, come in forty or more species. Parrot's feather, **Myriophyllum braziliense**, is one of the best known, with long feathery fronds.

Algae

Having briefly discussed plants, a few words about algae will not go amiss. Algae are primitive plants which soon colonize wet and aquatic environments. One only has to leave a glass jar containing clear water in strong light for a day or two, and a green deposit of algae will soon appear on the glass surface. In small quantities, green algae are not detrimental to the well being of the fish and other plants; indeed, they will contribute to the oxygenation and filtration, as well as provide food for browsing fish. Thread algae, or blanket weed, is a more serious threat, which grows in long filaments about the rocks and plants in the aquarium and, if not checked, will soon choke the other plants. Such algae can be thinned out at regular intervals by passing the fingers through the water, and gently pulling it out, taking care not to uproot the plants.

Blue-green algae is a sign of unhealthy conditions in a tank and, when it takes over, one may already have said goodbye to all the aquatic plants, if not the fish. Blue-green algae flourishes in alkaline water with much decaying matter. In such a case, the hold set up should be dismantled, sterilized and restarted from scratch, taking care not to allow conditions to redevelop as before. Brown or red algae is a sign of insufficient light in the tank. Algal growths on the inner glass surfaces can be scraped off using a special scraper or a razor blade. With a little trial and error experimentation, the patient aquarist will soon overcome the algae problem, once the correct balance of all the different factors has been attained.

The Water

Once the aquarium has been set up and planted, the tank can be filled with water. To prevent disturbance of the decorations, it is best to pour in the water gently via a flat dish, a sheet of glass or a piece of heavy brown paper. Once the tank has been filled, and the various heating, lighting and filtering apparatus set into motion, it should be left in this condition for a period of not less than fourteen days, before introducing any fish. During this time, routine checks on temperature and water quality should be made. If a green cloudiness, caused by floating algae, appears after a few days, this is no cause for undue worry as further maturation of the water will take care of this problem.

The quality of water in the aquaium is a complex subject and, as already mentioned, certain species of fish and plants will not adapt to conditions alien to their natural environment. Water may be hard or soft; acid, alkaline or neutral, depending on the type and quantity of mineral salts dissolved in it. Hard water is usually alkaline, and the majority of the world's tap water falls into this category. Hardness is caused by dissolved salts of mainly calcium and magnesium and is expressed in degrees of hardness (DH) as follows:

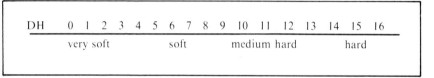

DH	0	1	2	3	4	5	6	7	8	9	10	11	12	13	14	15	16
	very soft					soft				medium hard				hard		

Various test kits are available which will indicate the amount and nature of dissolved mineral salts. General hardness can be measured using a hydrometer. Most freshwater fish require water which is reasonably soft but there are exceptions.

Acidity and alkalinity is measured on what is known as the pH scale, in which the figure 7 is neutral and the lower the number below 7 the more acid; conversely the higher the number above 7 the more alkaline. The tolerance range for most creatures is between 5.5 and 8.5 and only specially adapted organisms can be expected to thrive at a pH above or below this range. In general, the majority of aquarium fish and plants will live quite happily in a pH range of 6.5 to 7.5, which is close to neutral.

Before purchasing fish or plants, therefore, it is advisable to find out what the individual species require and plan your aquarium accordingly. Tap water can be converted to satisfactory aquarium water by using various buffer solutions to the manufacturer's instructions. A relatively new process developed after years of research, is the injection of carbon dioxide gas into the water at regular intervals which maintains acidity and provides nutrition for the plants. Aquaria using these systems always show lush, problem free plant growth and healthy fish. Aquarium science has indeed reached a stage where even the most difficult of species can be kept in an electronically controlled environment which reproduces the natural habitat in the minutest detail.

Test kits are available to measure the pH of water. The best type are those in which an indicator fluid is added to a sample of the water to be tested in a glass tube. The color of the resulting mixture is then compared against a color scale from which the correct pH can be read. Wherever possible, distilled water should be used for setting up an aquarium and in the consecutive topping up to replace water lost in evaporation. Where distilled water is not available, rainwater or tapwater which has been allowed to stand and then treated can be used. It will be of great value to visit your aquarist's supplier well before you set up your tank and ask his advice on the various products available. Although some products can be expensive for the beginner, a compromise situation can always be worked out.

3. General Maintenance

In a properly balanced aquarium, routine maintenance should take no more than a few minutes each week. A daily inspection is necessary to ensure that all systems are functioning correctly and this can be done at fish feeding time. Watch out for any dead fish or signs of disease in fish or plants so that treatment can begin at an early stage. Each week any sediment from food waste, fish excrement, or dead plant material which has collected on the surface of the substrate, should be removed with a siphon. Algae can be cleaned from the viewing glass with a scraper, and excessive plant growth can be pruned back. Water which has been lost through evaporation, or during the siphoning process, should be replaced, preferably with distilled or rain water. With regular care, an aquarium should not require dismantling and resetting up for at least two years.

Feeding

Before even discussing foods, it must be stressed that incorrect feeding is responsible for a major number of problems which may arise. Overfeeding appears to be a fault of many beginners and uneaten food laying on the aquarium bottom will lead to pollution in a very short time. Fish should be fed once or twice a day and never more than they can clear up in less than ten minutes. Large fish, particularly marines, should be fed individually, and any food that falls to the bottom of the tank removed immediately.

The number of commercially manufactured fish foods on the market is always on the increase and manufacturers are continually trying to improve their products. Foods come in the form of powder, for very small fish and fry, small and large flakes and pellets. Most are scientifically prepared and contain all the basic ingredients to provide a balanced diet for the fish they are destined for. This includes proteins, carbohydrates, fats, minerals and vitamins from animal and plant origins. High protein diets are available for carnivorous fish. For fish that consume powder or flakes, a mere pinch between thumb and forefinger is adequate for the average tank.

Although dried foods form a balanced diet, it makes a change for the fish to occasionally give them other items. Domestic foodstuffs provide a wealth of titbits which many fish will enjoy, but beware of overfeeding. Cooked potato, greens, spinach, peas and beans are useful vegetable foods. Small pieces of raw, lean beef, heart or liver are relished by carnivorous fish, as is cooked cod or haddock.

Live food is an important supplement to fish feeding and it enables some species to satisfy their hunting instincts as well as provide essential nutrients to breeding fish. Another advantage of some live foods is that overfeeding is less likely as any aquatic creatures used will continue to live until they are eaten. For small fish *Daphnia*, or water fleas are a good standby; they can be netted from small stagnant ponds and ditches and cultivated in a water butt. Called water fleas on account of their jerky movements in the water, *Daphnia* are really small crustaceans. The related one eye *Cyclops*, is another useful live food for small fish. Brine shrimp, the eggs of which can be purchased in small containers and hatched out at home in warm, aerated salt water, are ideal food for fry, small fish and, in particular, marine fish such as sea horses. Mosquito larvae, blood worm, and *Tubifex* are suitable for larger fish.

Of the non-aquatic live food, earthworms are probably one of the most nutritious and easily available. They can be dug up from damp soil and washed, before being fed whole, or cut into suitably sized pieces. Cultures of whiteworm and microworm can be purchased and further propagated in the home in small boxes, following the instructions of the supplier. Freshly swatted flies, mosquitoes and small moths can be fed to your fish, which will eagerly snatch such titbits from the water surface; however, flies which have been killed with aerosol sprays should never be used, for obvious reasons.

Health

The health of fish and other animals in the aquarium is directly related to the environment. Fish kept in less than optimum conditions will lose their natural resistance to disease organisms which are constantly present. Freshly imported fish, which have spent many harrowing hours in different containers and constant temperature changes, are particularly susceptible and great care should be taken when selecting fish for purchase. Preferably choose those that have been in the dealer's stock for a week or two and had a chance to partially acclimatize. Ensure that the fish are lively, uninjured and possess a healthy bloom. Fish are usually transported in plastic bags into which compressed air is introduced on top of the water. Such bags should be packed in polystyrene lined boxes, particularly in cold weather, and handled with care during transit. On reaching home the bags of fish are floated in the water of a quarantine tank to allow temperatures to synchronize. It is always adviseable to quarantine new fish for two or three weeks before introducing them to existing stock, thus reducing the chance of disease being brought in. Any fish in quarantine showing signs of ill health should be hospitalized and treated, or culled, depending on the severity of the disease or the value of the fish.

Diseases which may crop up from time to time include whitespot, *Ichthyophthirius*, which manifests itself as small white spots all over, or on parts of the head and body. The first sign is that fish will dash about and try to scratch themselves against rocks and other objects. Some excellent remedies are available from your supplier and treatment of the whole tanks's contents should take place as soon as possible. Velvet disease, *Oodinium*, which causes yellow, velvet like patches on the fishes' skin is a killer, but easy to treat if caught in time. Obtain *Oodinium* remedy from your supplier and use to the manufacturer's instructions.

Fungus diseases usually appear first on the fins and tail as white, streamer like growths, which later spread onto the body, destroying tissue in the process and eventually causing death, if untreated. It is easy to treat if caught in its early stages by immersing the fish in a solution of common salt, at a rate of one gram per litre of water. After two days, increase this to two grams per litre and prepare a fresh solution daily until all signs of fungus have disappeared. Reverse the process before returning the fish to its aquarium.

Certain external parasites can be a nuisance to fish and help reduce their resistance to other diseases. The anchor worm, **Lernaea**, is one such parasite, which is really a small crustacean that burrows under the skin. Proprietary cures are available. Another crustacean which can be a pest is the fish louse, **Argulus**, which attaches itself by its mouthparts behind the scales. It is thought to transmit disease from fish to fish as it changes hosts. To remove lice, catch up the fish, apply a small amount of spirit to the louse to make it release its jaws, then detach it with forceps and destroy.

Predatory insects may occasionally find their way into an aquarium through water plants or with *Daphnia*, such items as dragonfly larvae can be particularly voracious and will tackle quite large fish by sinking their powerful jaws into the flesh and sucking out the body fluids. The larvae and adults of various water beetles and some aquatic true bugs (Hamiptera) can be just as dangerous. Always keep a wary eye out for such dangers in your aquarium and remove with all haste if spotted.

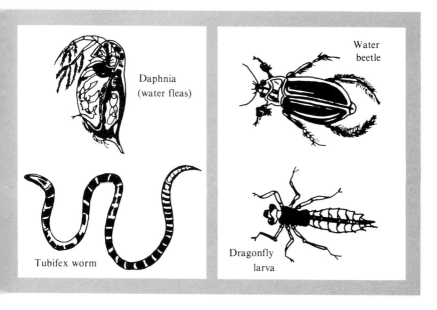

Daphnia (water fleas)

Water beetle

Tubifex worm

Dragonfly larva

4. Coldwater Aquaria

The only real difference between a coldwater and a tropical aquarium is that the former does not require any additional heating, usually being kept in the house, where the room temperature will dictate the temperature of the water in the tank. Fish kept in coldwater aquaria are, therefore, species from colder temperate climates which not only tolerate lower temperatures than most tropical fish, but are also able to withstand the seasonal temperature changes.

A Bubble-eyed goldfish. Most fancy varieties are more delicate than the common goldfish and are more suitable for indoor tanks than outdoor ponds.

A Veiltail goldfish.

The most popular of all coldwater fish, indeed perhaps the most widely kept fish of all, is the common goldfish. With a scientific name of ***Carassius auratus***, the wild variety is found in the slow moving watercourses of the Chinese mainland. Unlike its domesticated cousins, the wild goldfish is a sombre bronze-brown color but the ancestor of all the fantastic colors and forms of fancy goldfish to be seen today. The popularity of the goldfish is not difficult to understand; it is easy to keep and breed in captivity and is quite long lived, with specimens regularly attaining an age of twenty or more years. The common goldfish, of typical fish shape and red-gold in color, attains a length of about twenty centimetres, although aquarium specimens seem to regulate their growth according to the size of the tank. Most fancy varieties do not grow so large as the common goldfish and they tend to be delicate; more suitable for indoor tanks than outdoor ponds.

Above: Japanese bitterling
Rhodeus sericeus

Koi carp —
Cyprinus carpio

Some of the better known varieties include the comet; a streamlined fish with a forked tail as long as the body; the fantail, with its egg-shaped body and double tail fin; the lionhead, which lacks a dorsal fin and has a strange knobbly hood on its head, and the celestial, with eyes set on top of the head in such a way that it appears to be permanently gazing skywards. The shubunkin, is more typically fish-shaped but is attractively colored with a variegation of red, black and blue. The two main varieties of shubunkin are the London, which is similar in shape to the common goldfish, and the Bristol, which more resembles the shape of a comet. Other varieties include the telescope eyed, with its eyes set on the end of short stalks, and the moors which are jet black in color. Many of the fancy goldfish varieties are much prized by enthusiasts and there is great competition to produce the best specimens which can be rather expensive. Most are more delicate than the conventional types of goldfish and should be kept at a room temperature of not less than 15°C.

Other species of coldwater fish may not be as popular as the various goldfish varieties but nevertheless can be just as interesting. The common carp **Cyprinus carpio**, is suitable to keep as a youngster, but grows to an enormous size, some specimens in excess of thirty kilograms. Public aquaria often show such huge carp in massive tanks. A distinctive feature of carp, as compared with the goldfish, is the barbels situated in the corners of the mouth. Carp come in several varieties, including the mirror carp, with its large silver scales; the leather carp, which is almost scaleless, and the attractive golden carp. The tench, **Tinca tinca**, comes in two varieties, the green and the golden. Young tench are good additions to the aquarium and may be kept with goldfish. They are excellent scavengers and will eat food which falls to the bottom of the tank.

The orfe, **Leucistus idus**, is a good aquarium fish, but has a habit of jumping out of the water, so a secure cover must be used on the tank. Both the golden and the silver varieties are perhaps better suited to the garden pond as they grow larger. Various species of catfish are often available for the cold water aquarist but should be selected with care as most grow to an enormous size and will eat almost anything, including the other fish in the tank! The roach, **Rutilus rutilus**, and the rudd, **Scardinius erythrophthalmus**, are both colorful species with silvery bodies and reddish fins and are ideal community fish for the large coldwater aquarium or the outdoor pond.

The bitterling, **Rhodeus amarus**, and the three spined stickleback, **Gasterosteus aculateus**, are worth keeping in a small tank in order to study their interesting breeding habits; the former has an unusual relationship with the freshwater mussel, whilst the male of latter species builds a nest in which to rear the eggs and the young.

No book about fishkeeping can fail to mention the beautifully colored koi carp, a variety of the common carp which is really more suited to the outdoor pond, though young fish make an attractive addition to the aquarium. Some of the North American sunfish, such as the pumpkinseed, **Lepomis gibbosis**, are suited to the coldwater aquarium, but as they are aggressive, they are best kept with their own species only.

5. Tropical Aquaria

Perhaps the most popular type of home aquarium is that in which a community of colorful small tropical fish species are kept in a well decorated tank, with a lush display of aquatic plants. The choice of fish is immense, but care should be taken to select those species of a size, habit and compatibility for the type of aquarium to be created.

Some of the smaller members of the family Characidae from South America include the various tetras with their bright neon coloration. The neon tetra, **Hyphessobrycon innesi**, is one of the more popular types and its brilliant red and blue coloring is shown at its best if the fish are kept in small shoals of ten or more. The cardinal tetra, **Paracheirodon axelrodi**, is a similar species, but even more brightly colored. Other fish in the family which are usually available include the glowlight tetra, **Hemigrammus erythrozonus**, which has a brilliant red stripe along its silver body, and the serpae tetra, **Hyphessobrycon serpae**, in which the gray-green color is flushed with red, particularly by the male in the breeding season. Most of these species barely reach three centimetres in length and are at home in a slightly acid, well planted environment.

The family Cyprinidae contains over 1500 species including the goldfish and the carp. Many of the species possess barbels, or feelers, just below the mouth to help them find food in the substrate. Some of the smaller varieties are ideal community fish for the home aquarium. The cherry barb, **Barbus titteya**, reaches a length of five centimetres and is a silvery-fawn color with a dark brown stripe. The males show a cherry-red flush during the breeding season. One of the more popular species is the tiger barb, **Barbus pentazona**, with five broad, vertical, black stripes along the silver-gold abdomen. One of the larger barbs is the rosy barb, **Barbus conchonium**, with a maximum length of about fifteen centimetres. Being hardy and easy to breed, it is a favorite with beginners. Most of the barbs come from tropical Asia, and require acid to neutral water in a well planted tank. Other members of the family include the zebra danio, **Brachdanio rerio**, with attractive blue and silver horizontal stripes, and the similar but larger giant danio, **Danio malabaricus**. The harlequin, **Rasbora heteromorpha**, and the scissortail, **Rasbora trilineata** are two favorites amongst aquarists, both being small and colorful. The red-tailed black shark, **Labeo bicolor**, with its matt black body and deep red tail is another popular species.

The Cyprinodontidae, or egglaying tooth carp, are another family of fish with a fairly cosmopolitan distribution. Some of the better known species include the chocolate lyretail, **Aphyosemion australe**, which is a riot of color from

West Africa, the Ceylon panchax, **Aplocheilus dayi**, from Sri Lanka, in metallic green and blue, and another East African fish, the blue gularis, **Aphyosemion sjoestedti**, which has a reddish brown back, merging into blue-green along the sides and belly. All these fish require acid to neutral water, but another member of the family, the common killie, **Fundulus heteroclitus**, from the eastern coast of North America, requires hard alkaline water, with the addition of a little sea salt.

Neon and Cardinal tetra.

Below: Black neon and neon tetra in an attractive driftwood setting.

Tiger barb.

Middle: Ruby barb and Bleeding heart

Harlequin Fish.

Fish of the family Anabantidae are sometimes called labyrinths, due to the special organ adjacent to the gills which enables them to survive on atmospheric oxygen, when their waters dry up at certain times of the year. The gouramis are attractive fish with subtle coloring and exotic names to match, such as the moonlight gourami, *Trichogaster microlepis*, which is silvery blue, the pearl gourami, *Trichogaster leeri*, with its pearly scales and scarlet flush on the underside, and the dwarf gourami, *Colisa lalia*, a diminutive fish reaching five centimetres in length, brick red in color with blue-green vertical stripes. The jewel of the family, however, must be the Siamese fighting fish, of which there are several domesticated varieties. The males are bright red or blue with long flowing fins and have a reputation for being fierce; however, they are usually only aggressive towards males of their own species. Labyrinths have unusual breeding habits and build a bubble nest on the water surface in which to rear the eggs. The nest is fiercely guarded by the male. All species come from Asia and prefer acid to neutral water.

By far the most popular group of tropical fish is the family Poecilidae which contains the well known livebearers. These fish practice a primitive form of internal fertilization in which the sperm of the male is conducted into the female's vent via an appendage of the male's anal fin known as the gonopodium. The eggs develop full term in the female's abdomen and are borne as live fry. The most famous of the group is the guppy, *Poecilia reticulata*, which has many domesticated forms of shape and color, including such varieties as flagtail, lyretail and speartail. The molly, *Poecilia sphenops*, is another species with several varieties, including the famous black molly. The sailfin molly, *Poecilia latipinna*, is remarkable for its huge erectable dorsal fin, and the giant sailfin, *Poecilia velifera*, is even more spectacular, growing to about fifteen centimetres, with the erected dorsal fin of the male reaching five centimetres in height. The swordtail, *Xiphophorus helleri*, so named after the sword like appendage on the lower half of the male's tail, comes in many color varieties, is hardy and suitable for the beginner. All of the aforementioned livebearers prefer slightly alkaline water in a well planted tank.

There are many other families of tropical fish with species suitable for the aquarium. Hemiodontidae includes the interesting pencil fish, *Nannostomus*, and the Gasteropelicidae contains the bizarre hatchet fish species which hunt for insects at the water surface. The eel like kuhli loach, *Acanthophthalmus kuhli*, with its black and orange striped livery, and the clown loach, *Botia macracantha,* are two popular members of the family Cobitidae. Most tropical fish keepers like to have one or two specimens of catfish in their community tanks, some of which will act as scavengers and algae eaters. There are many species available from several families and one of the best is *Plecostomus*, the sucking catfish. The mailed catfish, *Callichthys*, and the leopard catfish, *Corydoras*, are popular species.

Zebra Danio.

Angel Fish

Leopard Catfish.

Above: The Guppy is a very popular fish.

Siamese Fighting fish.

Below: Golden sailfin molly.

Above: Wagtail swordtail.

Red-tailed black shark.

Below: Dwarf rainbow cichlid.

6. Marine Aquaria

It is possible to keep both cold water and tropical marine aquaria, but the latter is by far the most popular, probably due to the remarkable variety of color and interest associated with coral reef fish and invertebrates. Many public aquaria, particularly in coastal resorts, use natural seawater to display the local marine fauna, but for the home aquarium it is possible to manufacture artificial seawater from one of the excellent preparations supplied by marine aquarists' suppliers. Marine aquarium keeping is more complex than freshwater and this chapter can barely do more than scratch the surface of the subject, but it is hoped, will lead the reader into further investigation.

Substrate Materials

Washed coral sand, a mixture of powdered coral, mollusc shells and ordinary sand is normally used as substrate material in the marine tank. As an undergravel filter is often used, this should be installed first before adding a sloping layer of coral sand with a minimum depth of five centimetres. This substrate will be of considerable importance in the balancing function of the environment; as the set-up matures a host of minute organisms will colonize the gravel, and act as a biological filter, converting harmful waste products into relatively harmless compounds.

Decoration Materials

The most usual form of decorative material in a marine tank is the skeletal structures of dead coral. There are several types available with various bizarre shapes. The dead coral should be bleached, scrubbed and soaked in running water for several hours before use, when it will emerge brilliant white in color. The coral should be arranged firmly and decoratively in the tank. Living coral is occasionally available, consisting of thousands of polyps in a hard calceous skeleton which feed by catching micro-organisms with their tiny tentacles. 'Living rock' is another item which can be used, consisting of a piece of natural rock, complete with all its attached organisms taken from the marine environment. Many of the tiny invertebrates will soon colonize other parts of the aquarium and help create a balanced environment with a natural food chain.

Seawater

Seawater contains about three parts per thousand of mineral salts with slight variations from area to area, but consisting of about 65% sodium chloride (common salt), 16% magnesium sulphate, 12% magnesium chloride, 3% calcium chloride and the remainder split up into a large number of trace elements, each one of which plays an important part in the natural biological functions of marine organisms. Seawater is always slightly alkaline, with a pH between 7.9 and 8.5. Values above or below these are positively dangerous to organisms in the tank, so pH readings should be taken at frequent intervals. Overfeeding, or a dead fish in the tank, can soon create dangerously high pH conditions.

Packs of 'sea salt' can be obtained from your supplier and should be mixed with tapwater to the manufacturer's instructions. Once the tank has been set up with filter, gravel and decoration (other than living), a small amount of gravel from a mature marine tank should be added and then left for a period of at least fourteen days with filter and strong aeration running. This will allow bacteria from the mature tank to totally colonize the new gravel and set biological filtration into motion. Regular testing for pH, nitrite content and specific gravity should take place during this period, and no fish or invertebrates should be introduced until the correct conditions prevail. All the necessary testing equipment with instructions can be obtained from your supplier, who will also be able to advise you on various technical points.

Tropical seawater should be kept at a temperature of around 25°C with little variance day or night, summer or winter. Lighting should be strong, and broad spectrum tubes are recommended. Artificial lighting should have a twelve hour light/twelve hour dark cycle.

Marine Fish

Like tropicals, there is a multitude of species to choose from and room here to discuss a few only. Some of the damsel fishes of the family Pomacentridae are ideal for beginners; being adaptable they soon settle down in the marine tank. The domino damsel, **Dascyllus trimaculatus**, is black with a white spot on the head and one on each side of the body and attains a length of fifteen centimetres. There are several other damsels of similar size and a range of colors. The clown fishes, in the same family, with their unusual orange and white coloring, are always popular and fairly easy to maintain. They are famous for their symbiotic relationship with sea anemones, being able to live safely among the tentacles due to a chemical protection secreted from the fishes' skin cells. The common species is **Amphiprion percula**.

The surgeon fishes of the family Acanthuridae are another hardy group and include the powder blue surgeon, **Acanthurus leucosternon**, the clown surgeon, **Acanthurus lineatus**, and the gold rimmed surgeon, **Acanthurus glaucopareius**. All are very colorful and named after the sharp scalpel like appendage near the base of the tail. The butterfly fish of the family

Chaetodontidae are more difficult to keep due to their feeding habits. They feed on the coral polyps using their long, beak like snouts to delve into the tiniest crevices. Well known members of the family include the yellow butterfly fish, ***Forcipiger flavissimus***, which has a long pennant like extension to its dorsal fin.

Double-saddled butterflyfish.

Lionfish

Above: Black anemonefish.

Beaked butterflyfish.

Below: Blue damsel.

Some of the more bizarre species usually available include the lion or dragon fish, *Pterois volitans,* which has a reputation due to its poisonous dorsal spines and should be handled with caution. Sea horses of the family Sygnathidae are interesting aquarium inmates but must be given lots of small live food. A good species for the tropical tank is the golden sea horse, **Hippocampus kuda.** Puffer fish, some with spines, some without, are renowned for puffing themselves up with water when angry or afraid, increasing to many times their normal size. The spiny puffer, **Diodon holocanthus,** is useful for the community tank. Aggressive species, such as the trigger fishes of the family Balistidae, are best kept on their own as they will attack any other fish in the tank. One of the most unsociable varieties is the undulate triggerfish, **Balistapus undulatus.**

Most marine fish are carnivorous, either feeding on other fish or on invertebrates. Aquarium fish are usually fed on pieces of fresh shellfish such as prawns, cockles and mussels, or white fish such as cod or haddock. Many species will take live food only and can be given guppies (as they are easy and fast to breed) or other live food suitable for freshwater fish. Care must be taken not to overfeed such items as daphnia, mosquito larvae and tubifex which will not survive long in salt water and could be a source of pollution.

Useful Measurements

METRIC		BRITISH	U.S.
1 millimetre	=	0.03937 inch	
1 centimetre	= 10 millimetres	= 0.3937 inch	
1 metre	= 100 centimetres	= 39.3701 inch	
1 ..	= ..	= 3.2808 feet	
1 millilitre	= 1 cubic centimetre	= 0.0610 cu inch	
1 litre	= 1000 millilitres	= 1.7598 pints	2.1 pints
50 litres	=	11.0 gallons	13.2 gallons
100 litres	=	22. 0 gallons	26.4 gallons
250 litres	=	55.0 gallons	66.0 gallons
1 gram	=	0.035 ounce	
1 kilogram	= 1000 grams	= 2.24 lbs	

1 litre of water weighs 1 kilogram or approximately 2¼ lbs.
1 British gallon weighs 10 lbs = approx. 4½ litres.
1 American gallon weighs 9 lbs = approx. 4 litres.
30 centimetres are approximately 1 foot.
2½ centimetres are approximately 1 inch.
1 cubic foot of water is 6¼ gallons (British).